I WANT TO BE A
MARINE BIOLOGIST

Written by
Jonathan Reule

Illustration
Chong Wey Ming

Copyright © 2023 by Unibino Pte. Ltd.

All rights reserved. No part of this publication may be reproduced, stored in a retrieval system, or transmitted, in any form, or by any means, electrical, mechanical, photocopying, recording or otherwise without the prior written permission of the publisher or a licence permitting restricted copying.

First paperback edition August 2023
ISBN 978-981-17359-4-3

Published by Unibino Pte. Ltd.
31 Rochester Drive Level 3, #03-47 Singapore 138637

www.unibino.com

For ages, oceans, seas, lakes, rivers, and ponds have captivated our imaginations – not only for their beauty but also for what lives underneath the surface. If you've ever visited an aquarium, you'll know that there is an entire diverse world thriving underneath the waves. But how do we know about these many different creatures that inhabit our oceans, lakes and rivers?

Much of that is thanks to hardworking Marine Biologists, who make it their priority to study the many lifeforms living in these bodies of water. You see, Marine Biologists normally spend much of their time studying the ecology, behaviour, physiology, and genetics of marine organisms. It's not the easiest job, but those who give themselves fully to this profession find their rewards great.

Although you may be asking now how did this profession begin and why is it important in our modern world? There are several answers to these questions, but the best way to understand this is by jumping back in time to where our fascination first began with the underwater world.

It all started when we were still living in caves, stalking through the lands for food while evading predators who were on the prowl. At those times, our lives were very different than they are today. We didn't have grocery stores filled with food or restaurants spread throughout our towns. So we needed several sources of food to keep us alive - and that's just what we found in the lakes, rivers, and seas surrounding us.

This was when we started to explore these bodies of water to discover what other resources they might be holding. It didn't take us long to realise there was more underwater than meets the eye. We began harvesting other items, such as sea sponges, algae, clams and molluscs. We soon found that these organisms could be used for a host of purposes.

For example, sponges could be used to help scrub dirt from our bodies. Clams could be cooked in our meals, while their shells could be used as jewellery or even digging tools, thanks to their unique shape! As you may be able to tell, living near the water and using it as a resource helped us survive those trying years as a species.

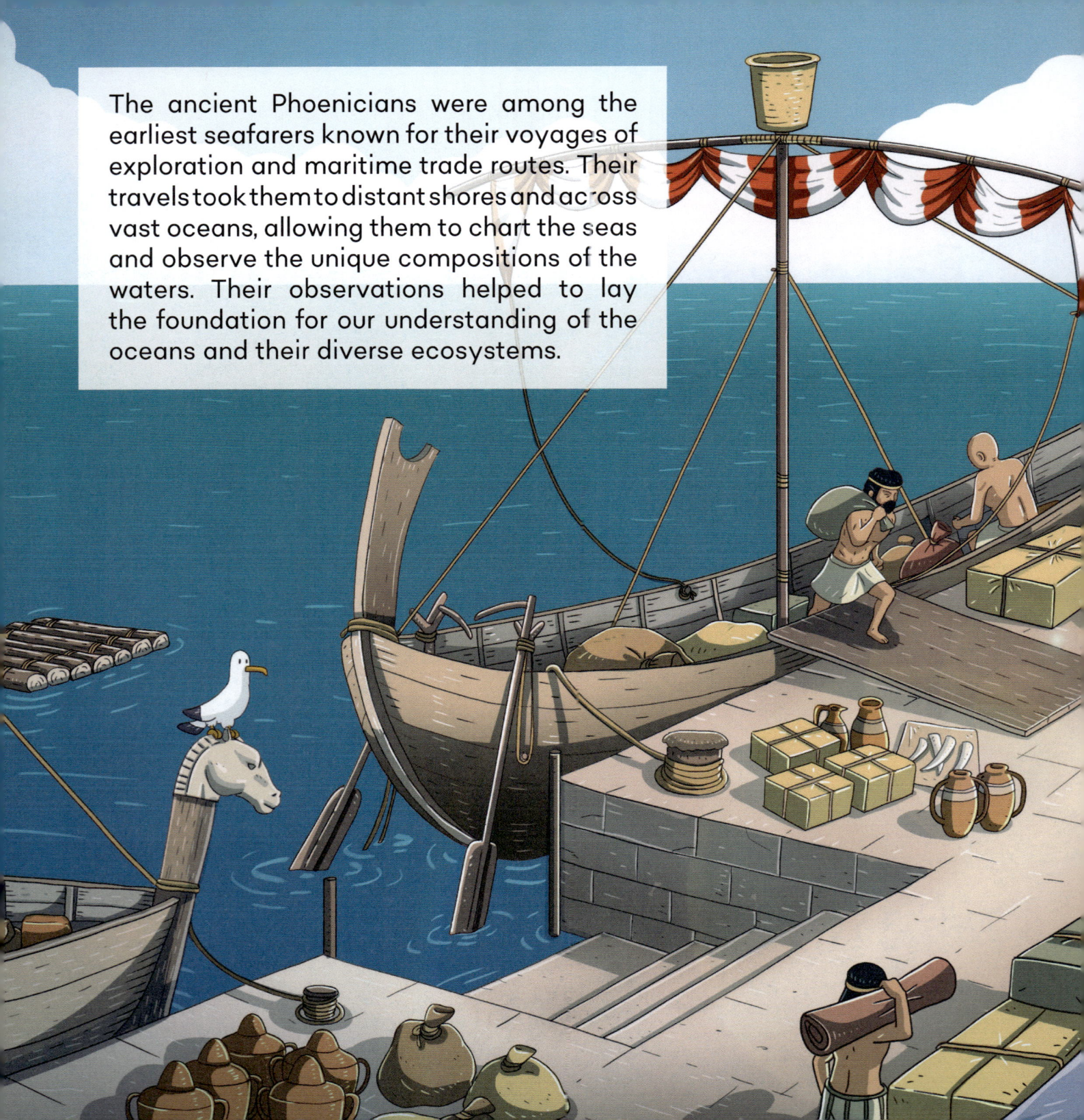

The ancient Phoenicians were among the earliest seafarers known for their voyages of exploration and maritime trade routes. Their travels took them to distant shores and across vast oceans, allowing them to chart the seas and observe the unique compositions of the waters. Their observations helped to lay the foundation for our understanding of the oceans and their diverse ecosystems.

In particular, the Phonecians were especially known at that time for selling murex shells, which were often used to help dye garments royal purple. Their trading and use of murex shells not only demonstrate the Phoenicians' understanding of marine life but also highlight their early contributions to the field of marine biology.

However, the formal study of marine life can be traced back to ancient Greece, where Aristotle made recorded observations of the habitats of marine creatures in his work History of Animals during the 3rd century BC. In his work, he documented hundreds of different types of sea creatures, including fish, octopuses, sharks, and sea urchins. But that wasn't all he discovered.

He also correctly identified that some species of whales give birth to live young and that dolphins are mammals, not fish. Through his work, he also helped to devise the classification system for animals - a key element to marine biology that is still used today! Although he wasn't always right, and the classification system has changed over the years, he still was a visionary of his time.

However, it wasn't until many years later that the oceans and seas were explored to a greater degree. During the mid-1800s, the age of discovery began. Th s was a period when many nations were making larger boats and using these vessels to travel farther than before.

There were many new sea creatures discovered on these journeys. Although several are hard to believe existed. Take, for example, some medieval maps that show giant sea dragons attacking ships. Or how about massive crawfish snapping a human in its pincer? And one of the more bizarre features of a boar-headed fish, with eyes on the side of its body!

Another notable contributor to this field is Edward Forbes, who is often referred to as the father of modern-day marine biology. In the 1800s, he was given a grant to go to the British Virgin Isles, where he conducted a rigorous study of the starfish in that region. He made records of more than 100 starfish, drawing each by hand!

As time progressed, the science of Marine biology was established as a genuine discipline around the world. In 1872, the British sent out one of the first-ever research ships to study the oceans without any other purposes. It was common during those ages for expeditions to be military missions, with some research performed on the side.

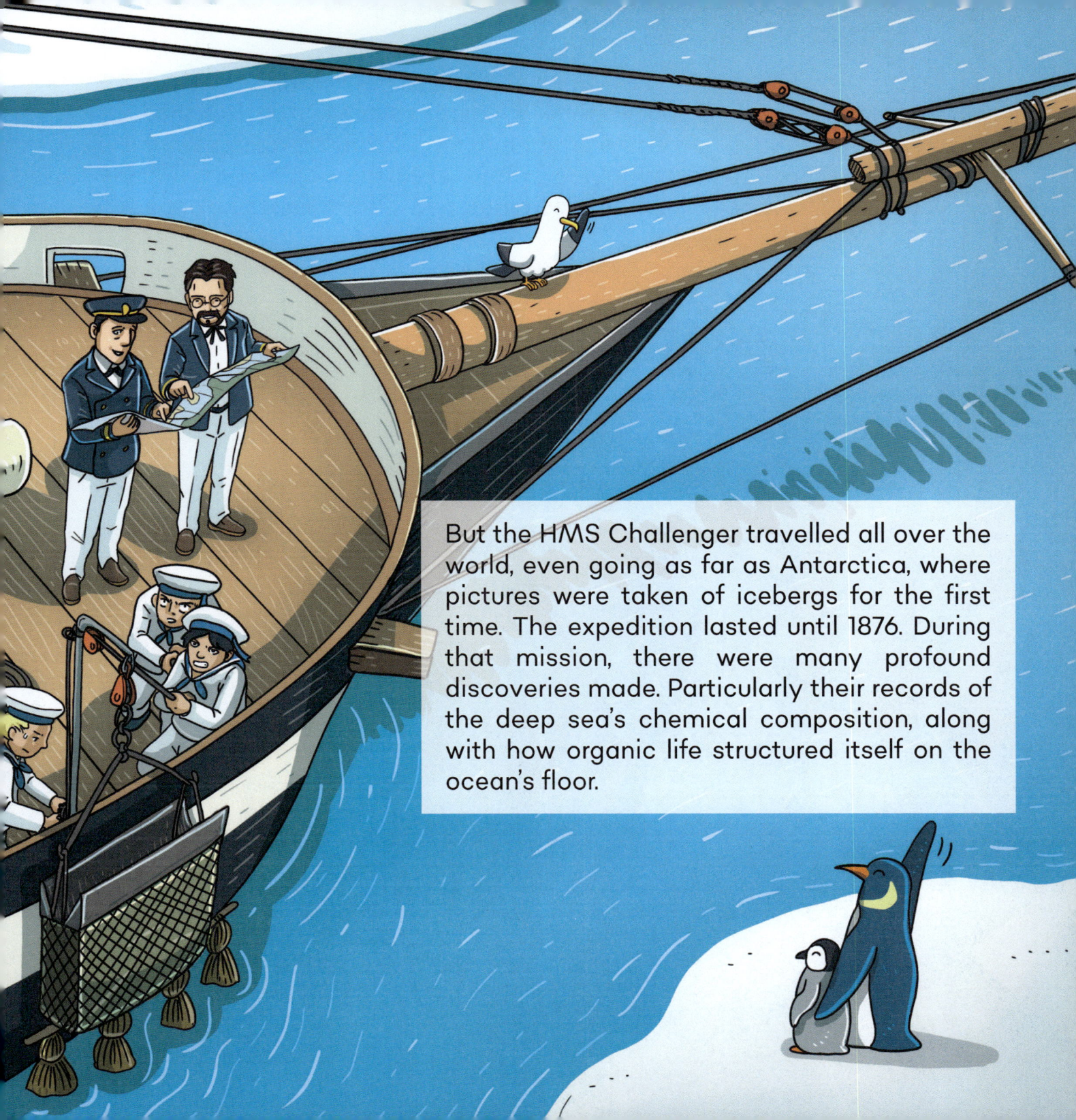

But the HMS Challenger travelled all over the world, even going as far as Antarctica, where pictures were taken of icebergs for the first time. The expedition lasted until 1876. During that mission, there were many profound discoveries made. Particularly their records of the deep sea's chemical composition, along with how organic life structured itself on the ocean's floor.

All of these great studies are what constructed the foundation for modern-day Marine Biology — that and the many great technological advancements that came in the 19th century. From scuba gear to submersible crafts, our ability to research the oceans and their depths became much more accessible.

Not only that, but soon, nations started to build their own Marine Biology Laboratories, where they could conduct studies without going to sea. The first international research centre was constructed in Woods Hole, Massachusetts, in 1888. And since then, it has expanded into a massive centre, with more than 250 employees and 500 visiting scientists every year.

But this may have you wondering how to become a Marine Biologist yourself. Well, it's important that you enjoy studying marine life, from seaweed to coral and the various types of fish in the oceans. Next, you should prepare yourself in college by getting a degree in biology, or better yet, finding a program that specialises in marine biology!

All of these great studies are what constructed the foundation for modern-day Marine Biology — that and the many great technological advancements that came in the 19th century. From scuba gear to submersible crafts, our ability to research the oceans and their depths became much more accessible.

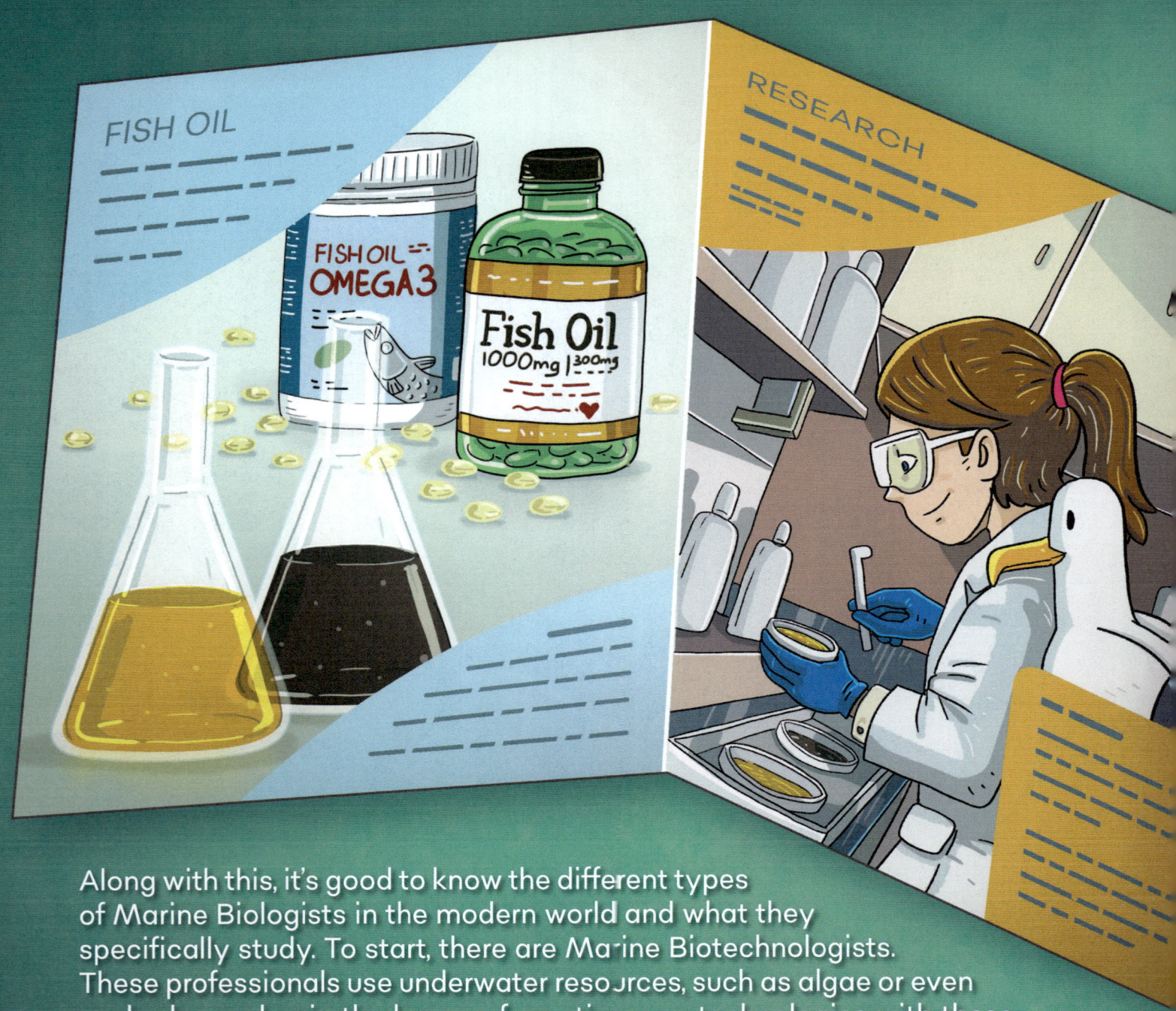

Along with this, it's good to know the different types of Marine Biologists in the modern world and what they specifically study. To start, there are Marine Biotechnologists. These professionals use underwater resources, such as algae or even seabed samples, in the hopes of creating new technologies with these elements. You may find them working with pharmaceutical companies, using certain marine properties to help make new effective medications.

Fish biologists, or ichthyologists, are specialists who work primarily with fish and other sea creatures in the oceans. They may focus their career on learning more about certain types of fish or even trying to find undiscovered species hiding in the vast oceans. Fisheries can also consult Fish Biologists to make sure that the populations remain healthy in their farms on a daily basis.

Whereas population biologists are concerned with the amount of fish in the sea, quite literally. These scientists study the population of marine organisms, determining not only their behaviours but also where they live and whom they share their habitats with. Population biologists can often be found in the wild, collecting data and analysing populations to track their natural movements as a group.

Benthic biologists are another vital profession within the Marine Biology umbrella. These researchers study the various organisms living on the seafloor to determine the health of bodies of water. They often work by collecting what are known cs Benthic invertebrates - which is a fancy word for animals such as worms, lobsters, crabs, snails and some aquatic insects! You'd be surprised how much information these little critters can give to researchers about the health of these habitats.

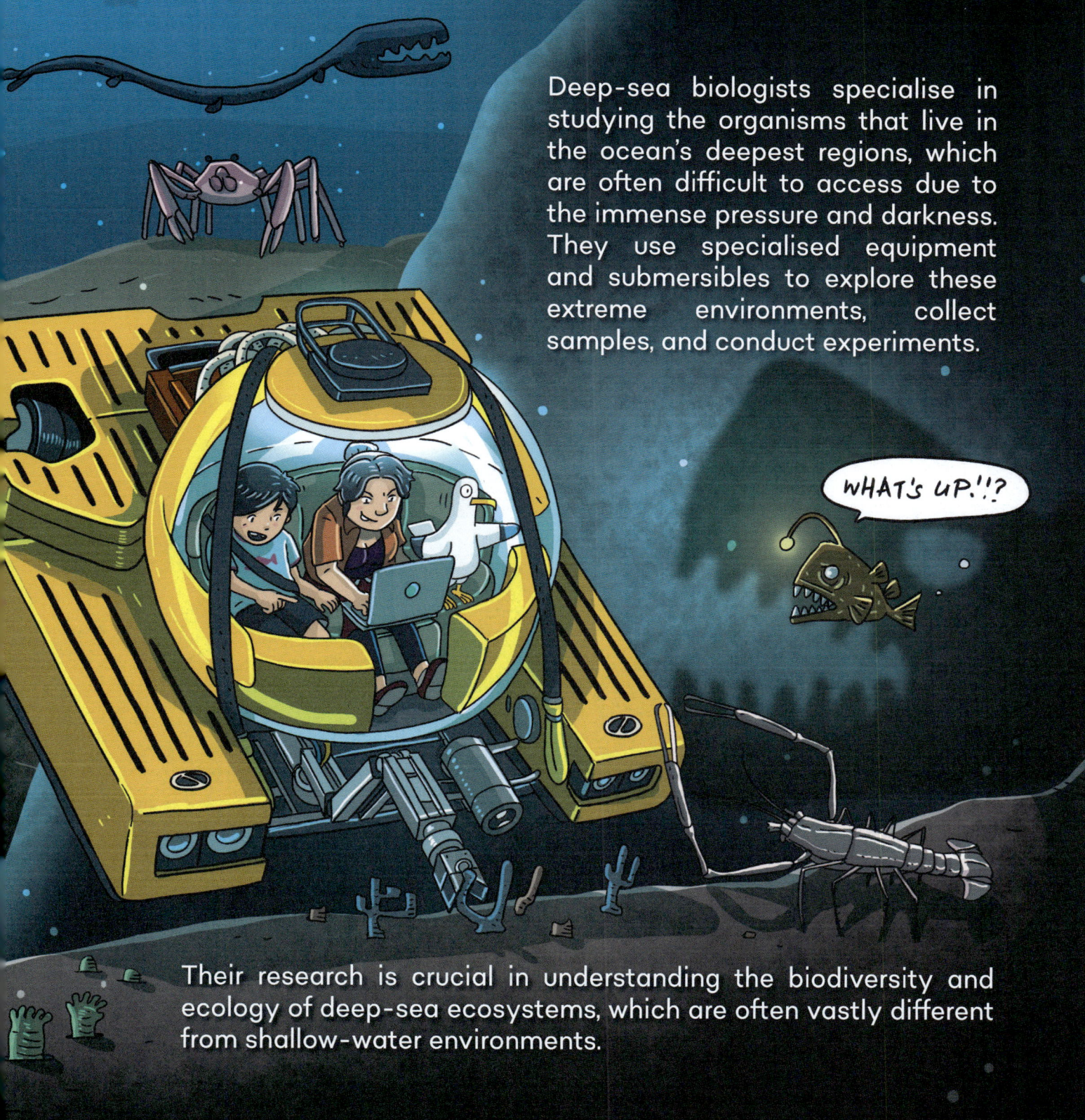

These aren't the only possibilities for marine biologists though! There are plenty of other opportunities for those who choose to make a career within this field. Some become veterinarians, helping specifically with aquatic animals, while others may go on to manage an aquarium where a wide range of sea creatures are kept!

But no matter which particular job you decide upon in Marine Biology, it's important that you take your studies seriously because this field requires the use of math on a regular basis.

It is also essential that you are brave enough to take a boat out to sea and that you are a confident swimmer as well. From time to time, you may find yourself going on a dive with scuba gear too, and carrying lots of equipment for your projects.

As a marine biologist, you will be able to contribute to the understanding of the complex and interconnected systems of the ocean. Your work could lead to important discoveries about marine life, such as the discovery of new species or identifying environmental problems underwater. You could also be involved in conservation efforts to protect endangered species and ecosystems.

In addition to the scientific benefits, a career in marine biology can also be personally fulfilling. The opportunity to work closely with marine life and ecosystems can be incredibly rewarding, and the chance to make a difference in the world can be a powerful motivator. With a career in marine biology, you can truly make a positive impact on the world and help to ensure the health and sustainability of our oceans for generations to come.

My Inspiration

Shubhi Saxena
Founder, Unibino

As a parent in this ever-changing world, it can sometimes feel overwhelming when it comes to our children's futures. New technologies seem to be arising almost every day, and with so many innovations, it creates unique professions which many of us wouldn't have dreamed to be necessary only a few years ago. Which to me is a good thing. Because with so much variety, my children can have the opportunity to pick a career that will fit their personalities and build upon their strengths. As you may imagine, this desire within me to provide my children with the resources they needed to thrive, led me to search out books that would be easy enough for them to understand while teaching them about various professions.

Only, I found that these books were few and far between. Even if I could find a book about a certain profession geared towards young readers, I found them sparse inside and limited to only certain careers that may not fit my children's abilities. This is when I came up with the idea to write my own children's books, teaching them about all the various careers in the modern world. After months of researching different professions and learning more than I ever expected, I quickly realised this was going to be a bigger project than I first anticipated. I dove into the histories of these professions, discovering links to the past, and why these professions were now so important.

Ultimately my goal was to offer my children options, to show them that there is no one set path for everyone. But in this, I stumbled upon something bigger. I wanted to share this with future generations. To share with all children and parents about these careers, to help spark curiosity, and to instil a passion for the future. Everyone has special talents and abilities, and I hope that this series will be able to offer clarity and inspiration to children around the world. Because at the end of the day, it's never too early to start dreaming and never too late to take action. With this, I hope you enjoy this series and that your young ones become the best versions of themselves as they can achieve.

Printed in Dunstable, United Kingdom